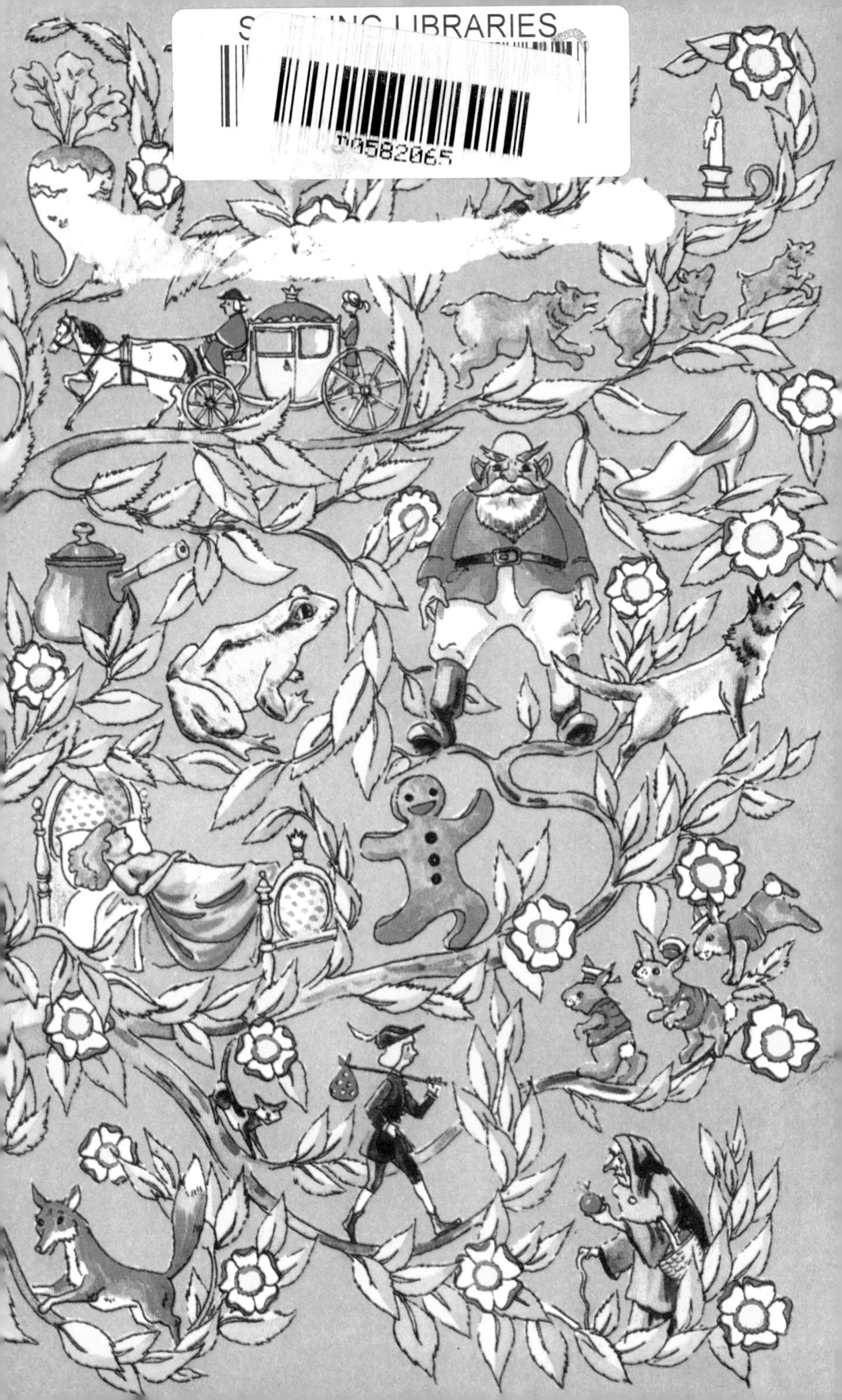

This *LADYBIRD TALE*
belongs to

....

The Three Billy Goats Gruff

Retold by Vera Southgate M.A., B.COM
with illustrations by Frank Endersby

LADYBIRD 🐞 TALES

ONCE UPON A TIME there were three billy goats called Gruff.

One fine day, the three billy goats Gruff set off up the hillside. They were going to look for some sweet grass to eat.

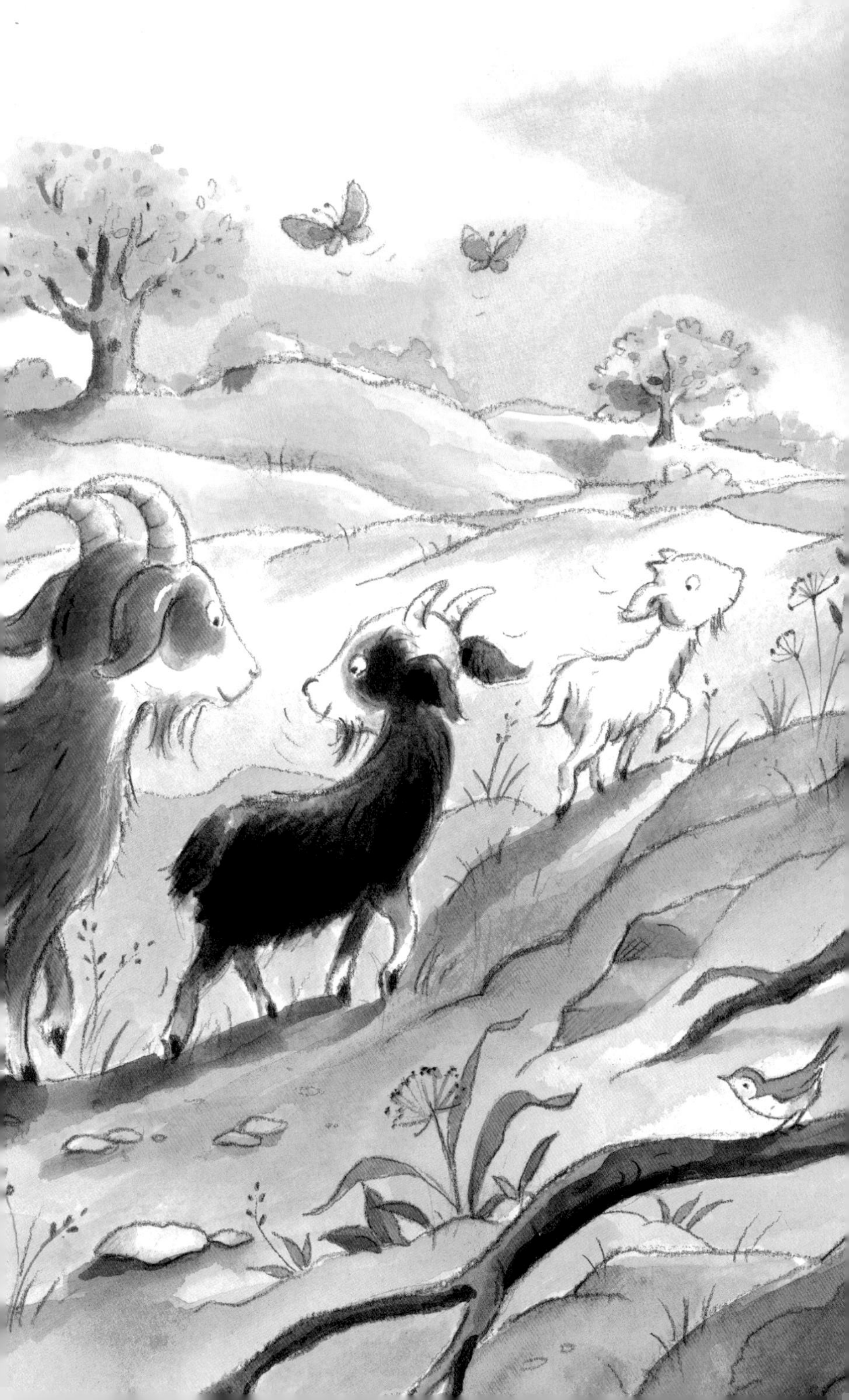

On the way up the hillside, the three billy goats Gruff came to a river.

On the other side of the river was a beautiful meadow. In the meadow was the finest grass they had ever seen.

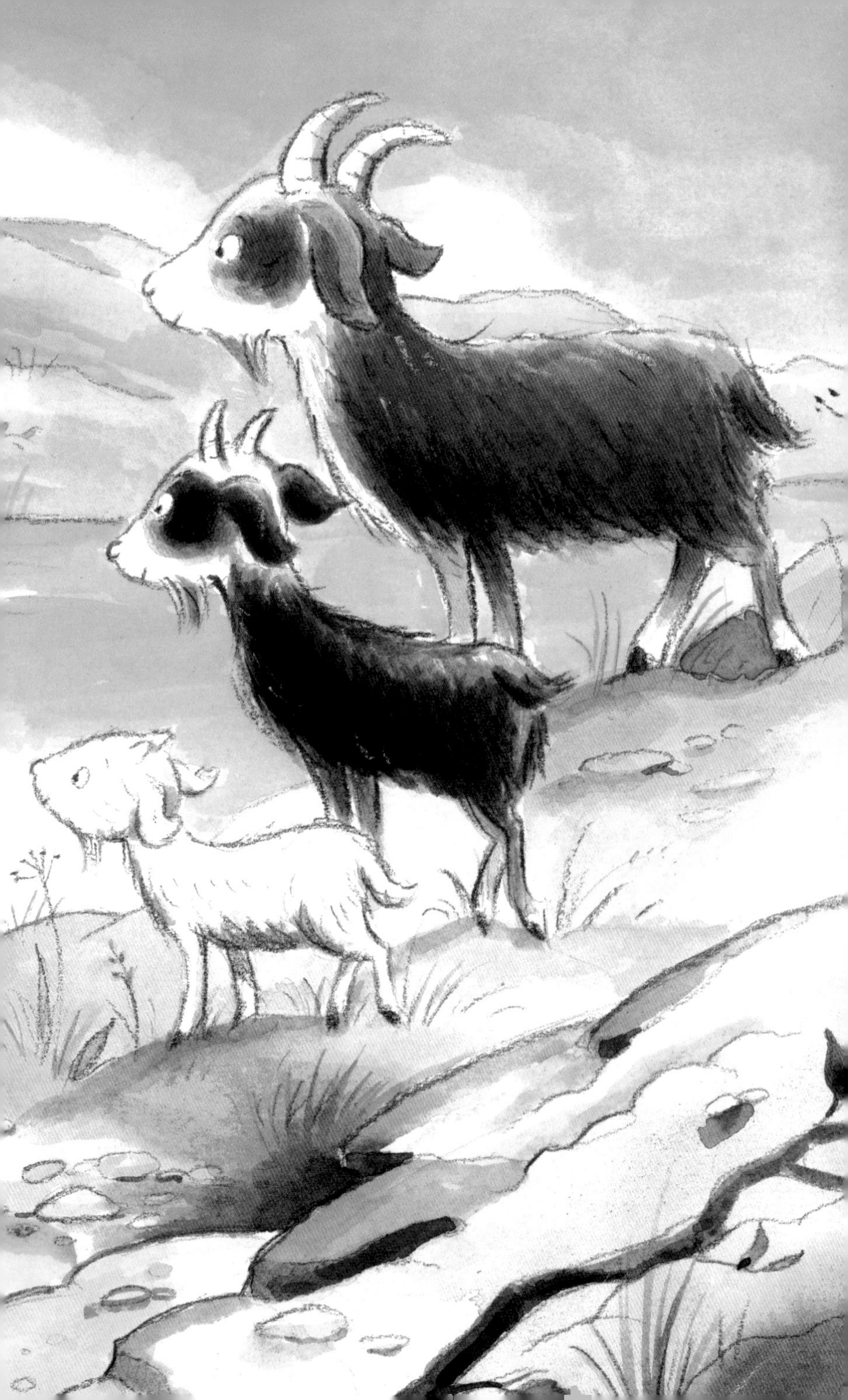

There was a wooden bridge over the river, but under the bridge there lived an ugly troll. People were afraid to cross the bridge because of the troll.

Every time he heard footsteps on the bridge, he popped out and gobbled up the person who was trying to cross.

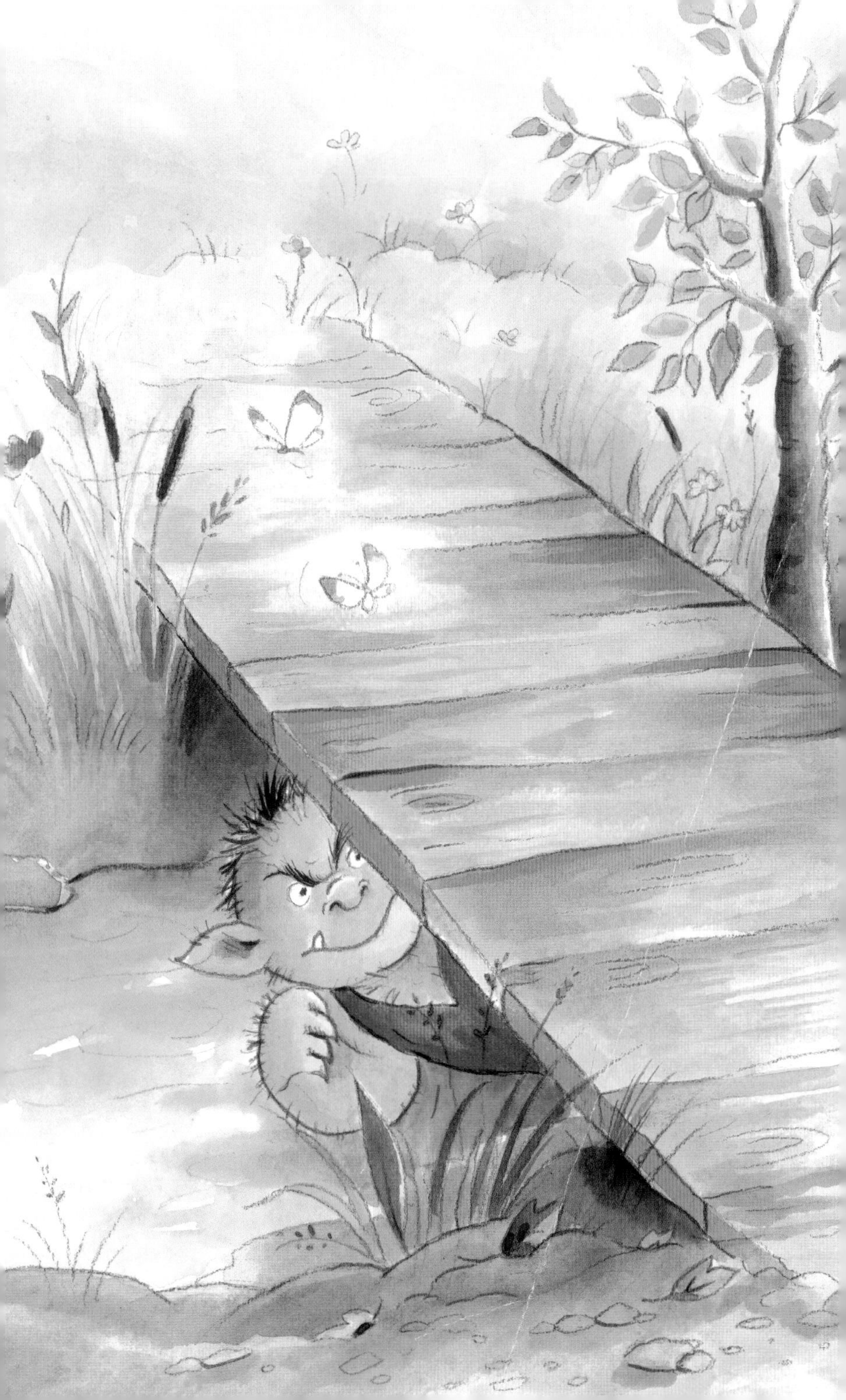

The three billy goats Gruff were very frightened at the thought of the troll. Yet they longed to eat the sweet grass in the meadow on the other side of the river.

After a while, the youngest billy goat Gruff said that he would be the first to try and cross the bridge.

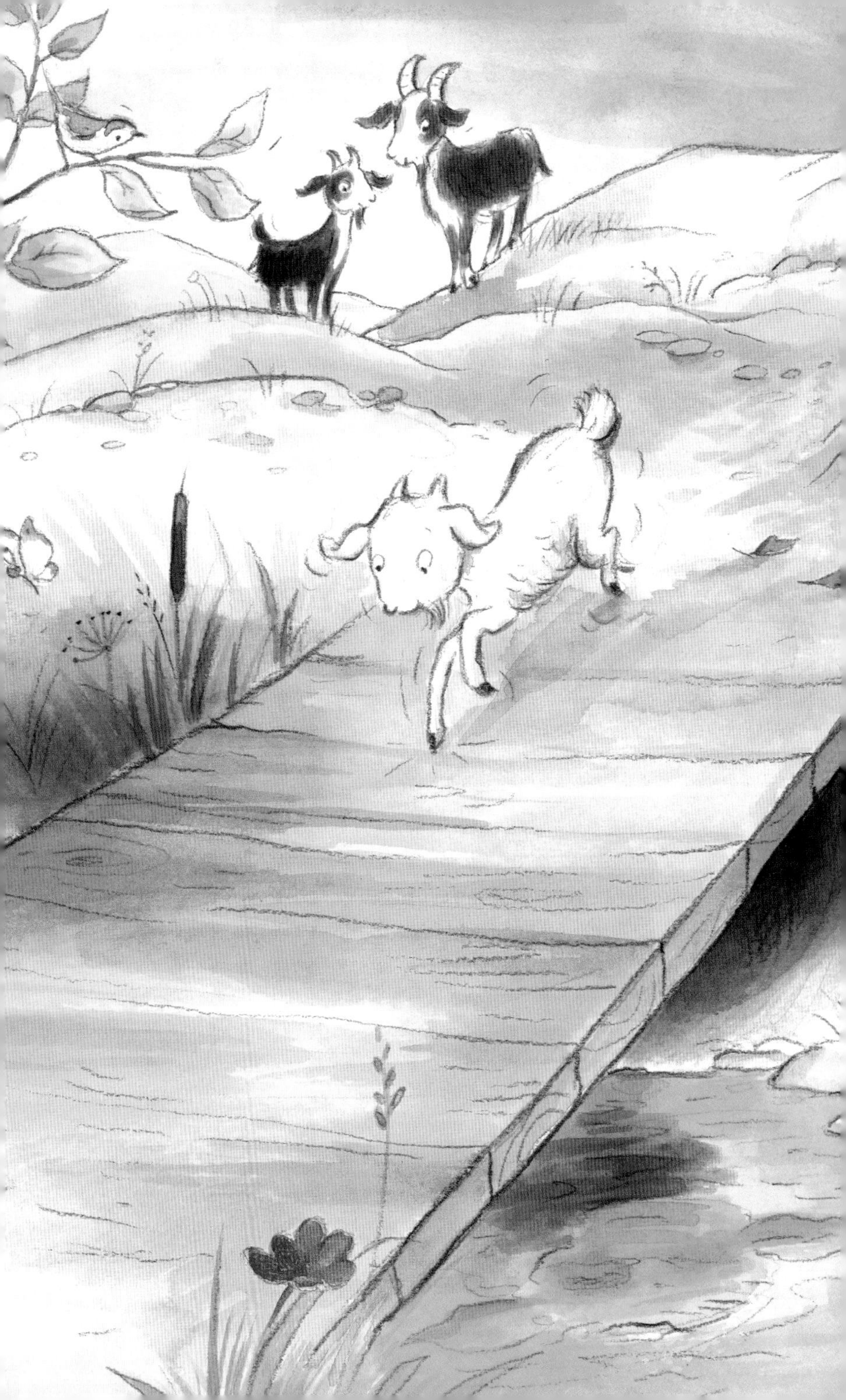

Trip, trap, trip, trap went the hooves of the youngest billy goat Gruff on the wooden bridge.

Out popped the troll's ugly head. He was so ugly that the youngest billy goat Gruff nearly fell down with fright.

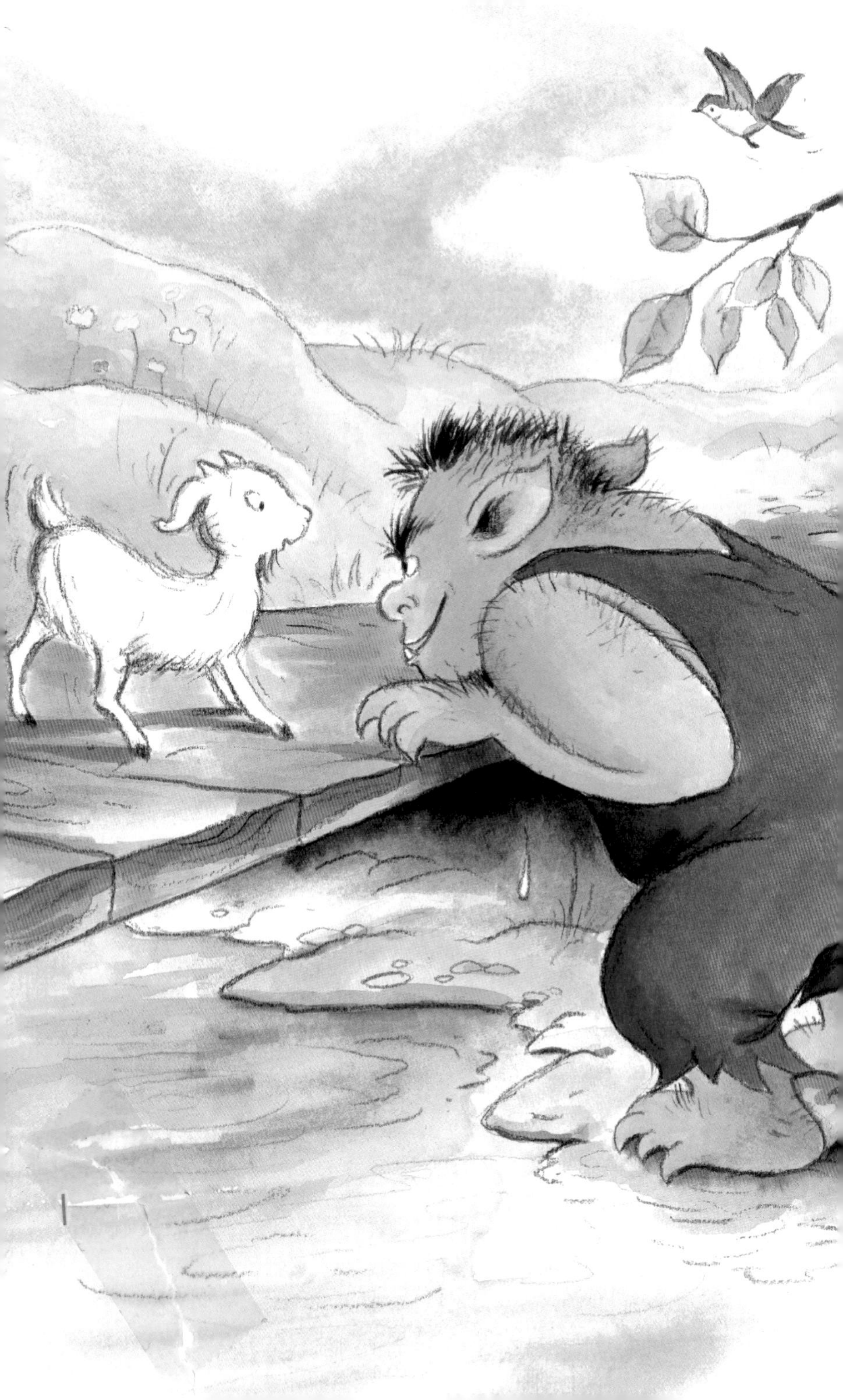

"Who's that trip-trapping over my bridge?" roared the troll.

The youngest billy goat Gruff spoke in a tiny voice. "It's only me, the littlest billy goat Gruff," he said. "I'm going to the meadow to eat the sweet grass."

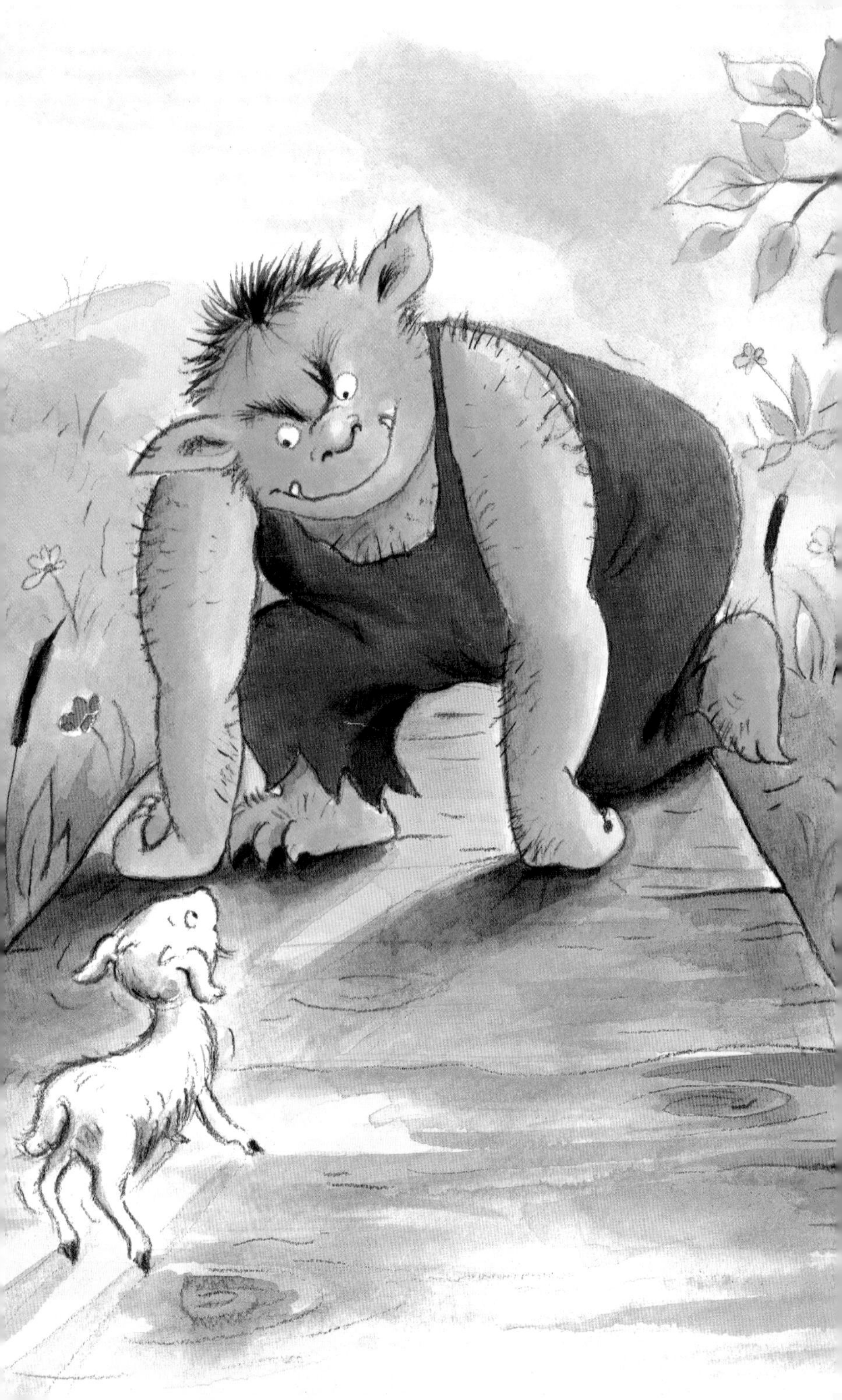

"Then I'm coming to gobble you up," roared the troll.

"Oh no! Please don't gobble me up," said the youngest billy goat Gruff in a tiny voice. "I'm far too little and not at all tasty. Wait until the second billy goat Gruff comes along. He's much more tasty than I am."

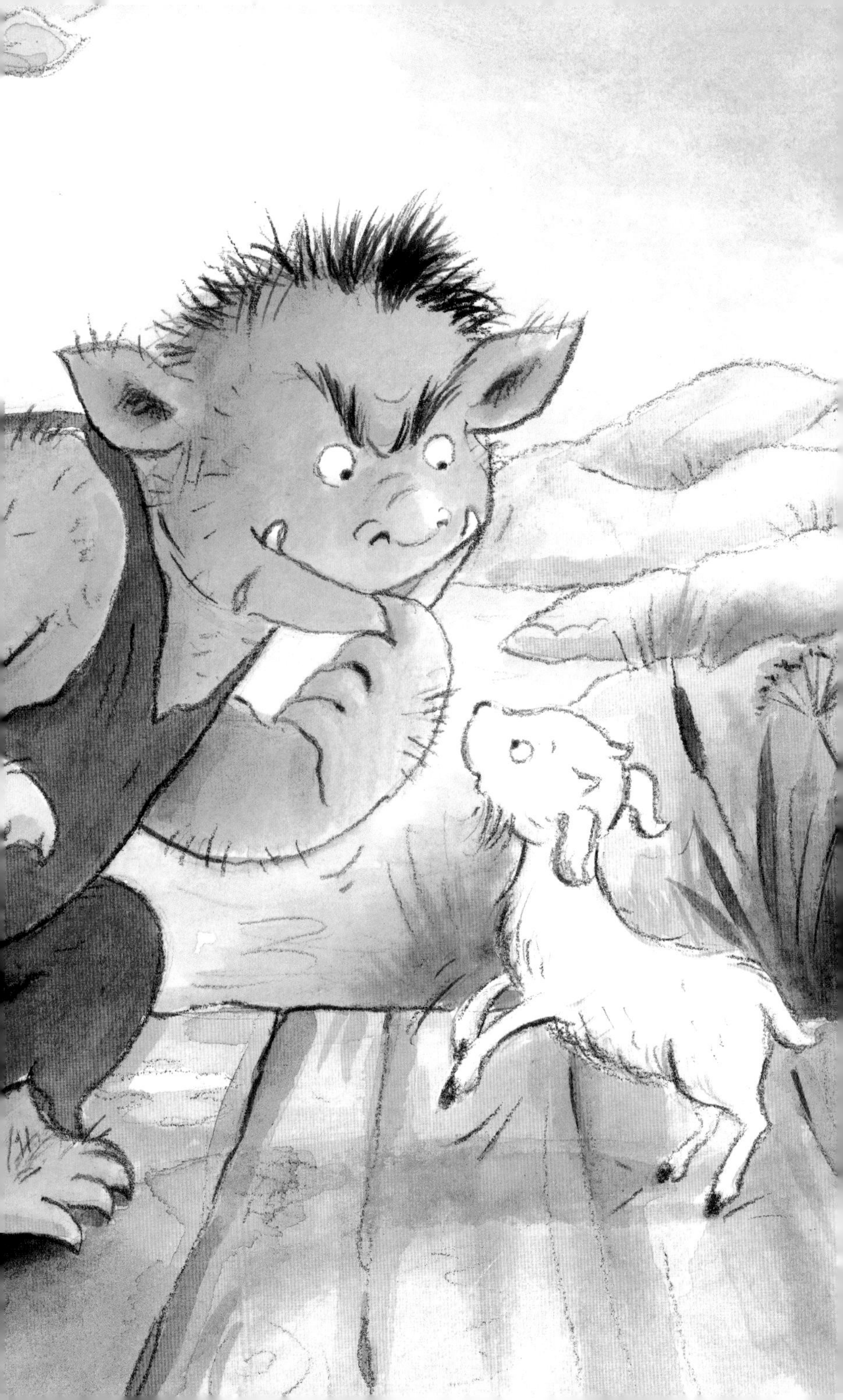

"Very well," said the troll. "Be off with you! I'll wait until the second billy goat Gruff comes along."

So the youngest billy goat Gruff crossed the bridge and skipped off into the meadow to eat the sweet grass.

Then the second billy goat Gruff said that he would try to cross the bridge.

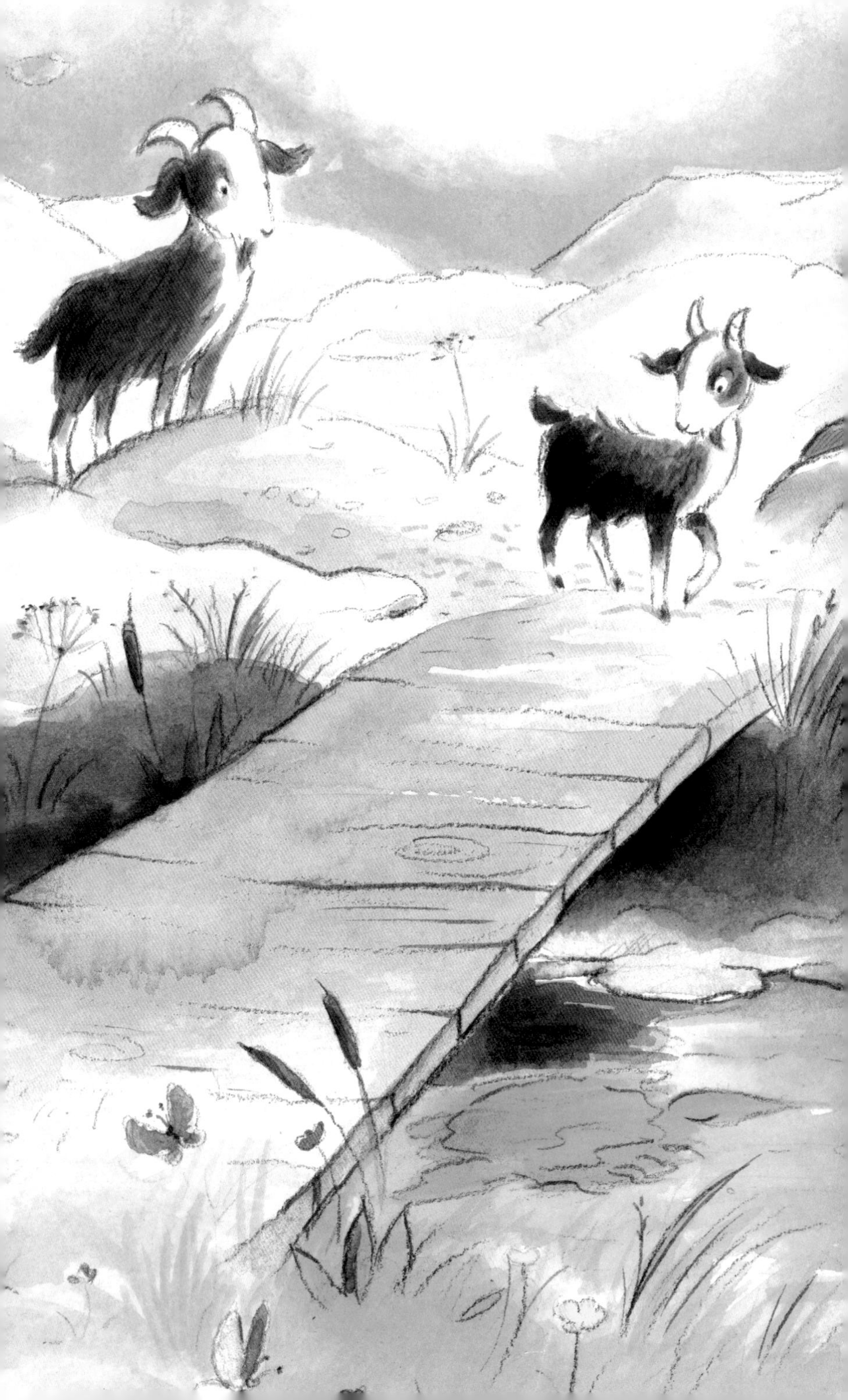

Trip, trap, trip, trap went the hooves of the second billy goat Gruff on the wooden bridge.

Out popped the troll's ugly head. He was so ugly that the second billy goat Gruff nearly fell down with fright.

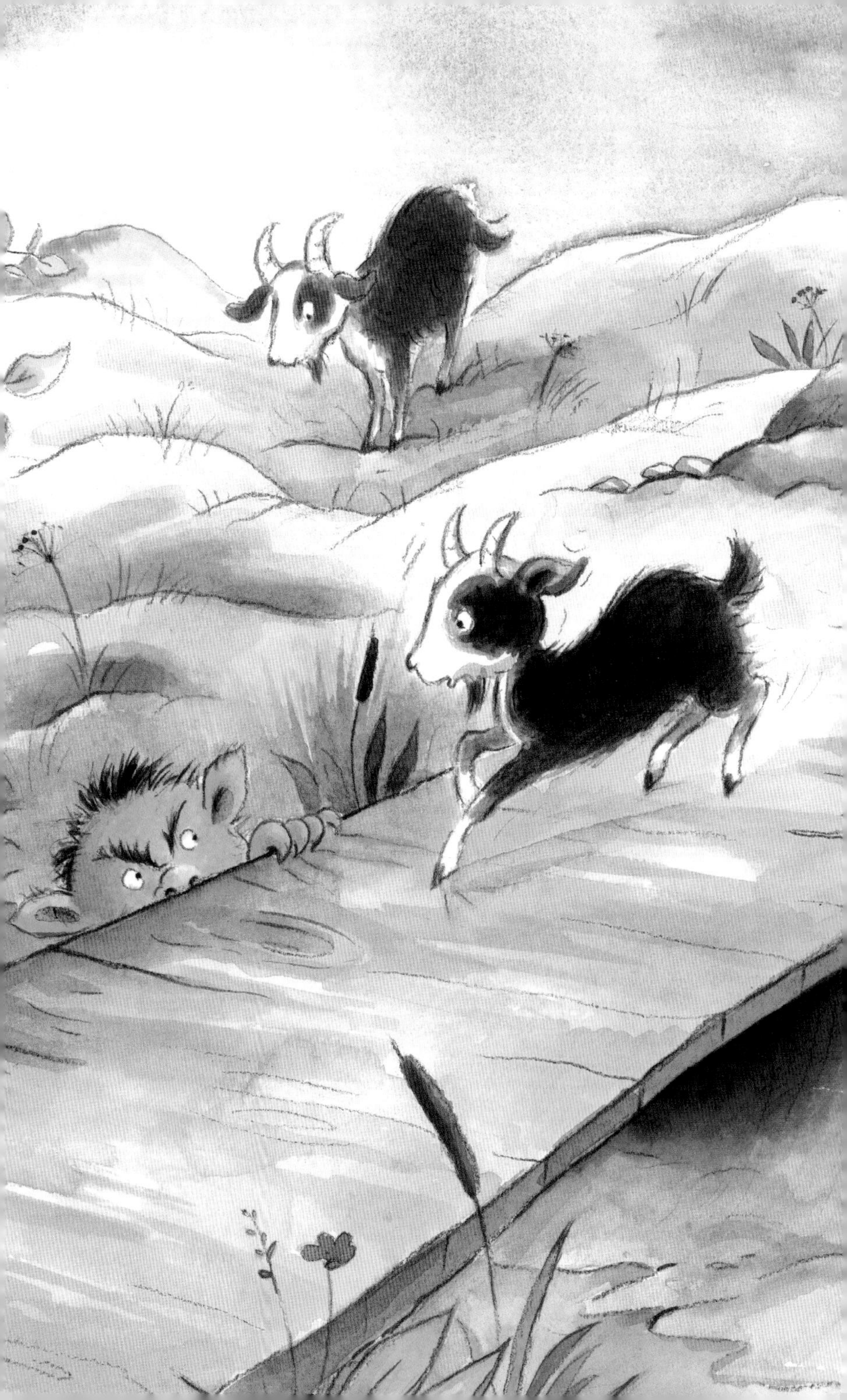

"Who's that trip-trapping over my bridge?" roared the troll.

The second billy goat Gruff spoke in a rather soft voice. "It's only me, the second billy goat Gruff," he said. "I'm going to the meadow to eat the sweet grass."

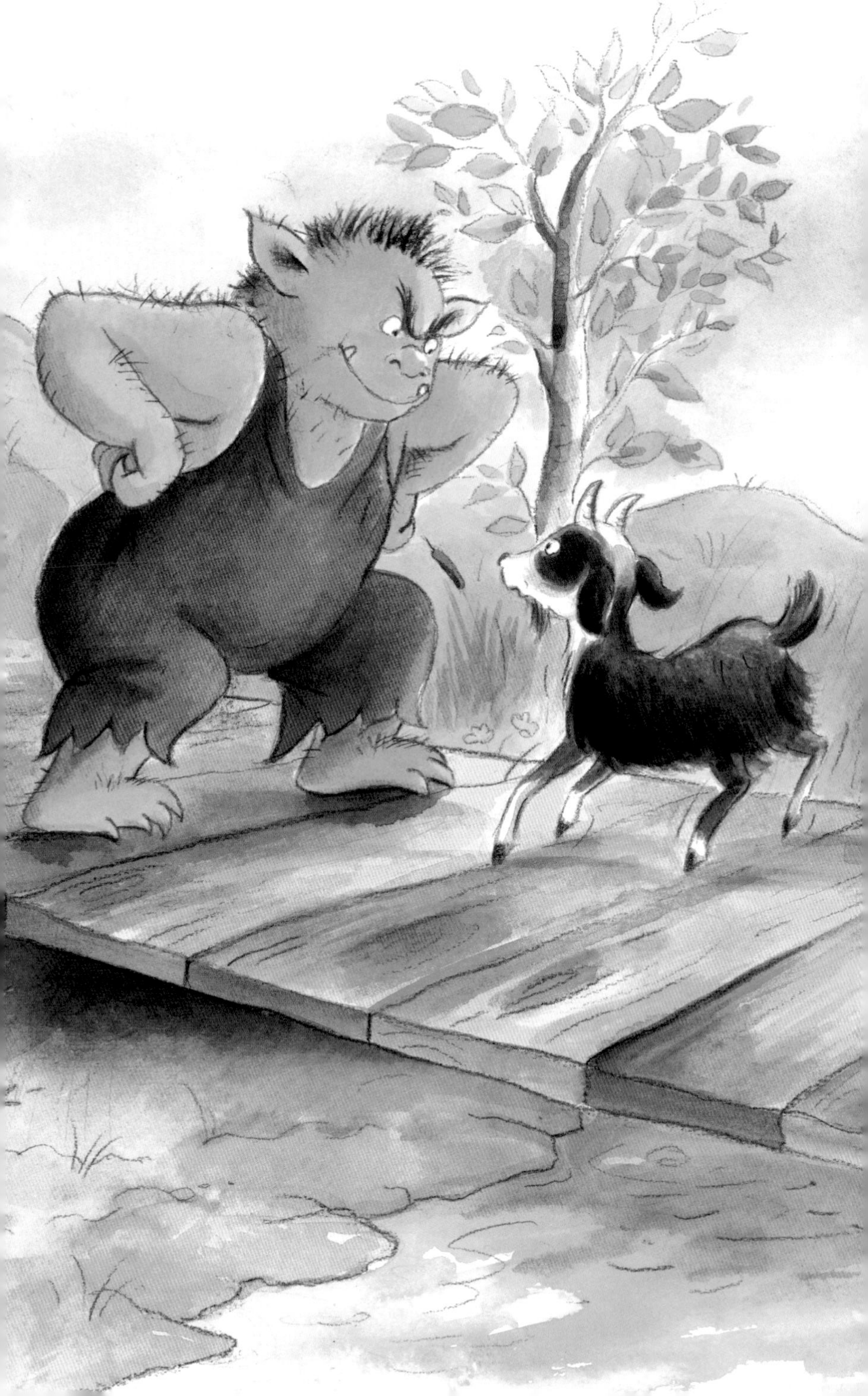

"Then I'm coming to gobble you up," roared the troll.

"Oh no! Please don't gobble me up," said the second billy goat Gruff, in his rather soft voice. "I'm not very big and I'm not very tasty. Wait until the third billy goat Gruff comes along. He's very big and very tasty."

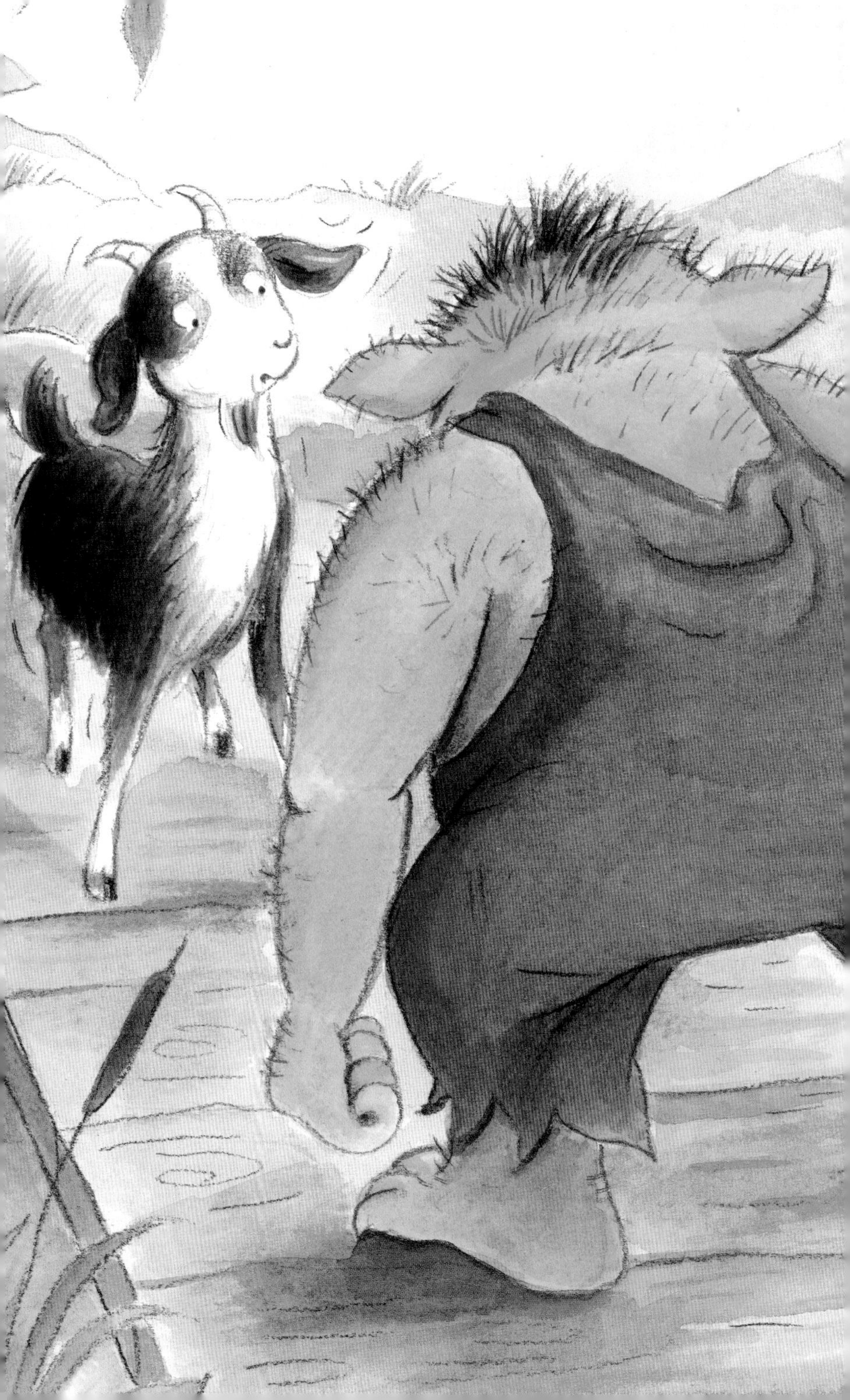

"Very well," said the troll.
"Be off with you! I'll wait until the third billy goat Gruff comes along."

So the second billy goat Gruff crossed the bridge and skipped off into the meadow to eat the sweet grass.

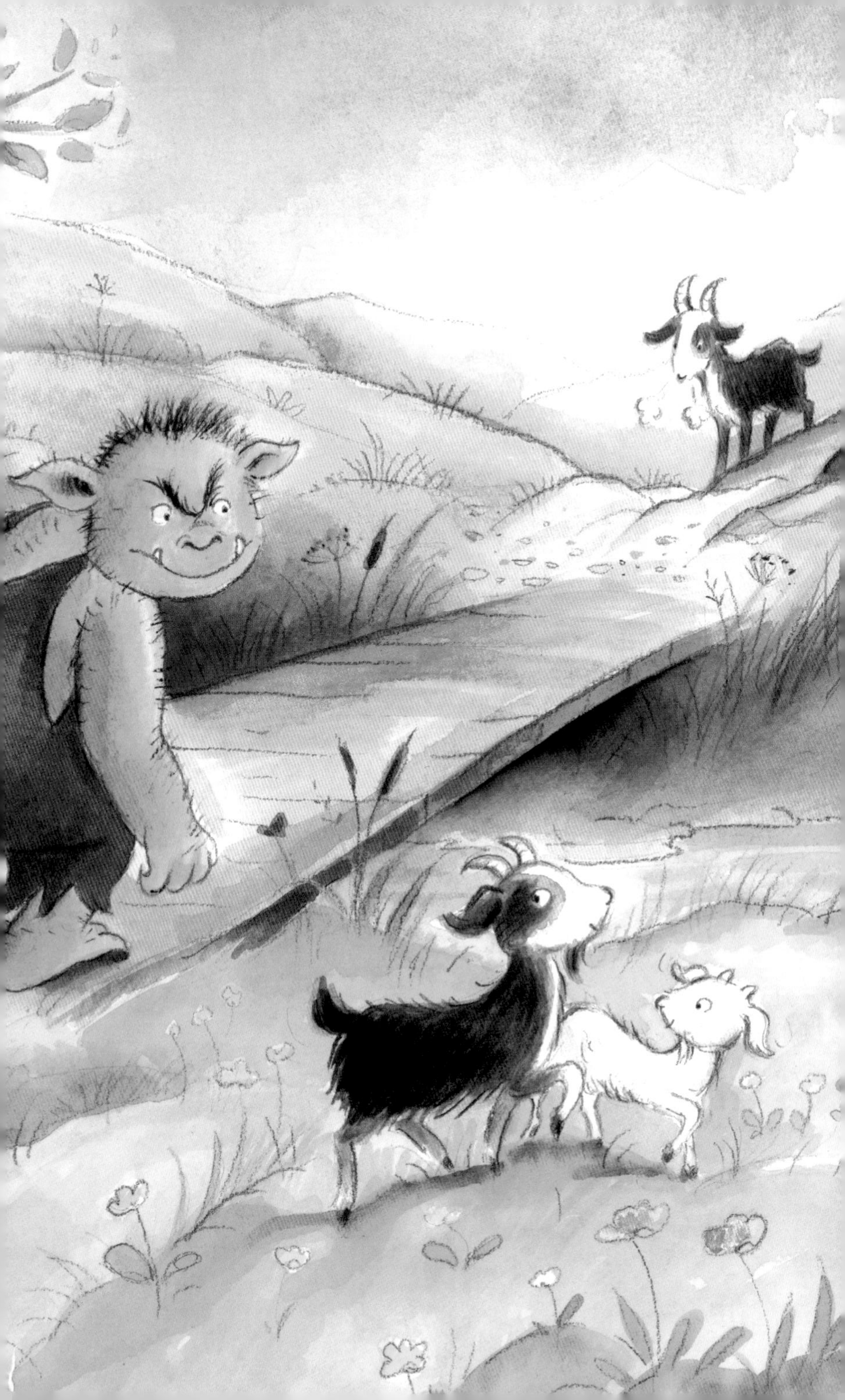

Then, at last, the eldest billy goat
Gruff came up to try to cross
the bridge.

He was a very big billy goat.
His beard was long and his horns
were almost fully grown.

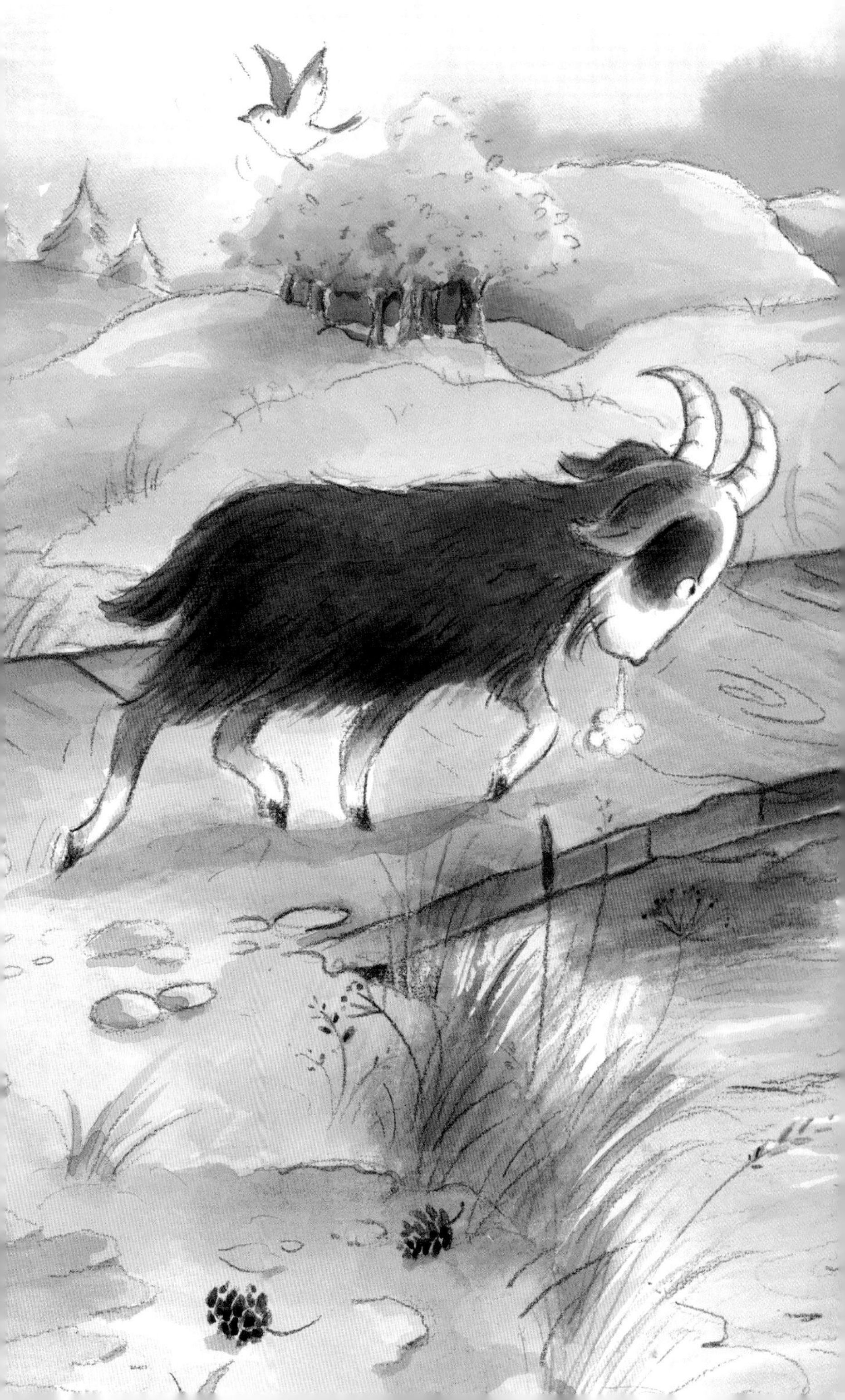

TRIP, TRAP,
TRIP, TRAP,
BANG, BANG,
BANG, BANG,

went the hooves of the eldest billy
goat Gruff on the wooden bridge.

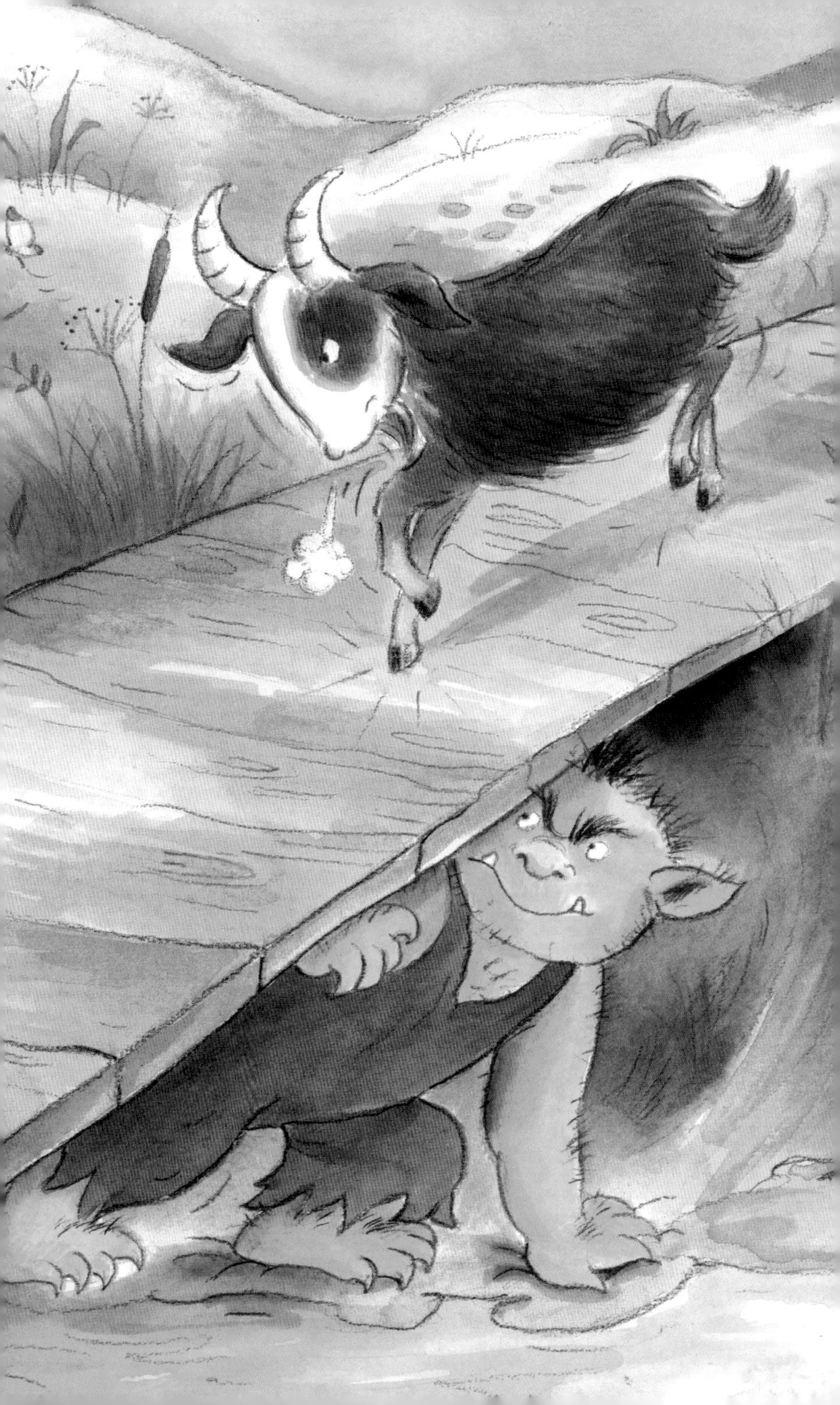

Out popped the troll's ugly head. He was so ugly that the eldest billy goat Gruff nearly fell down with fright.

But he did not show it. He only stamped his hooves harder:

TRIP, TRAP,
TRIP, TRAP,
BANG, BANG,
BANG, BANG!

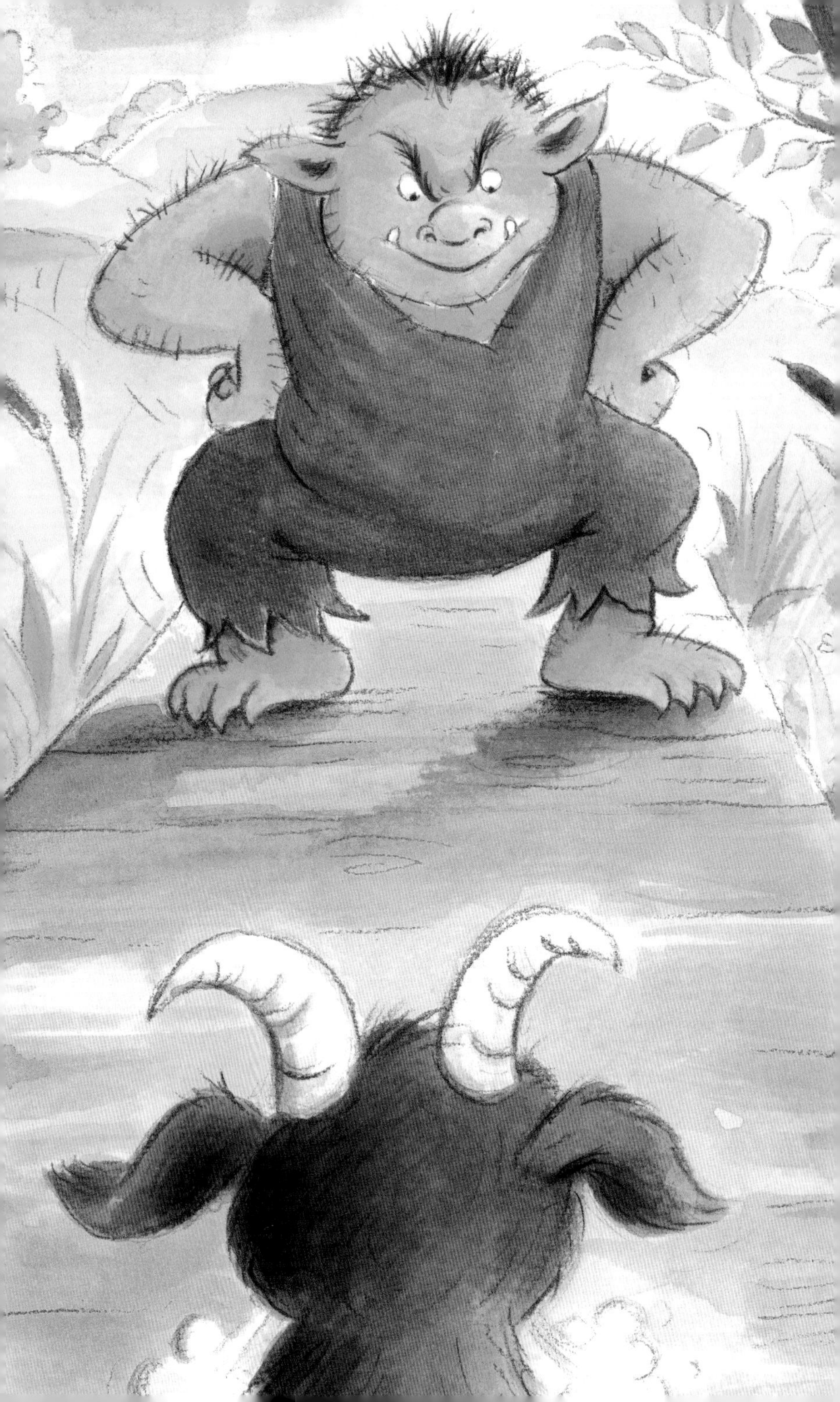

"Who's that trip-trapping over my bridge?" roared the troll.

The eldest billy goat Gruff's voice was even louder and gruffer than the troll's voice. "It's me, the biggest billy goat Gruff," he bellowed.

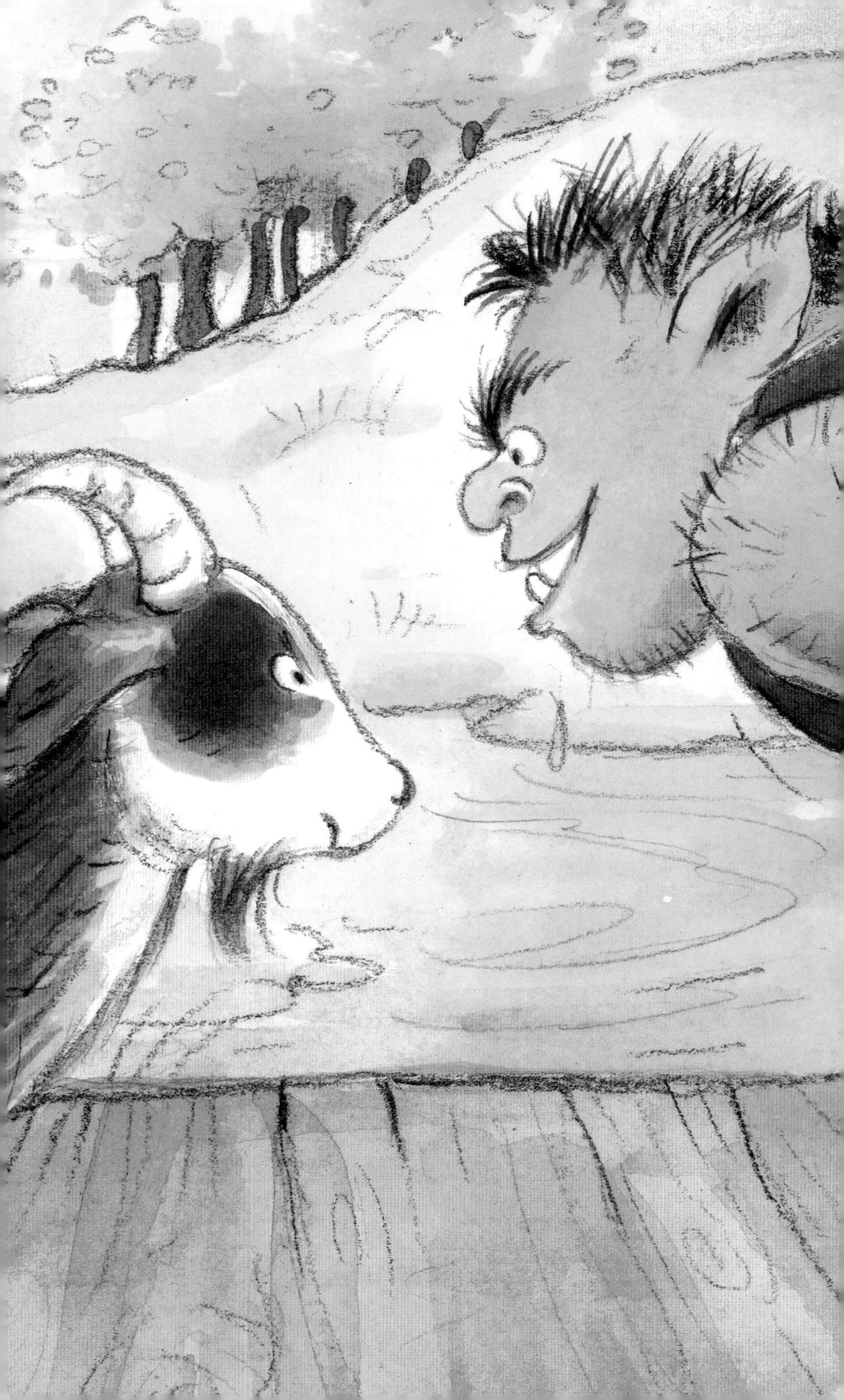

"Then I'm coming to gobble you up," roared the troll.

"Oh no, you are not!" bellowed the eldest billy goat Gruff. "I am coming to gobble you up!"

And he stamped his feet even louder:

TRIP, TRAP,
TRIP, TRAP,
BANG, BANG,
BANG, BANG!

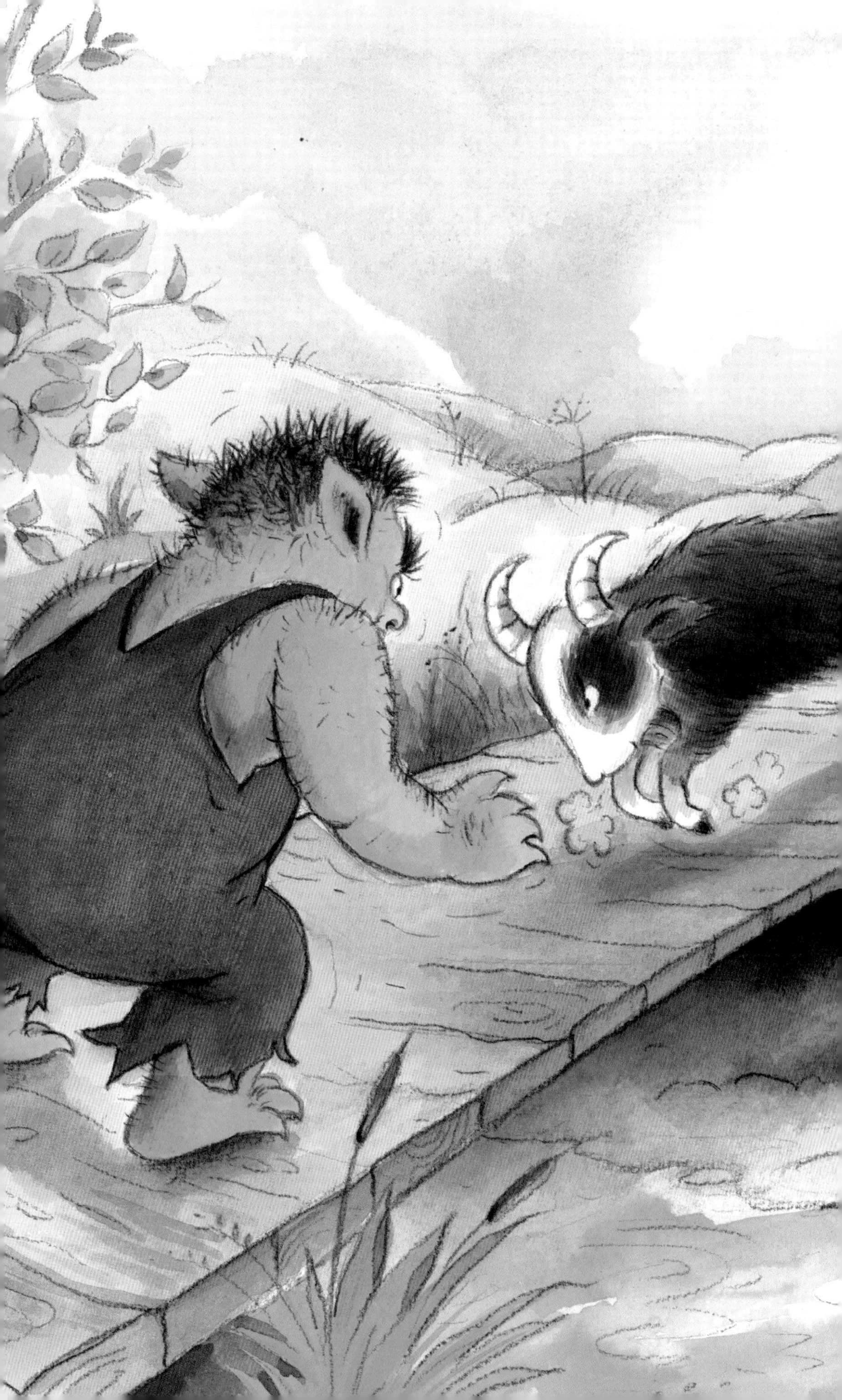

After that, the eldest billy goat Gruff butted the troll with his big horns.

The ugly troll fell off the bridge head first into the deep water. There was a mighty splash and the troll disappeared, never to be seen again.

So that was the end of the ugly troll.

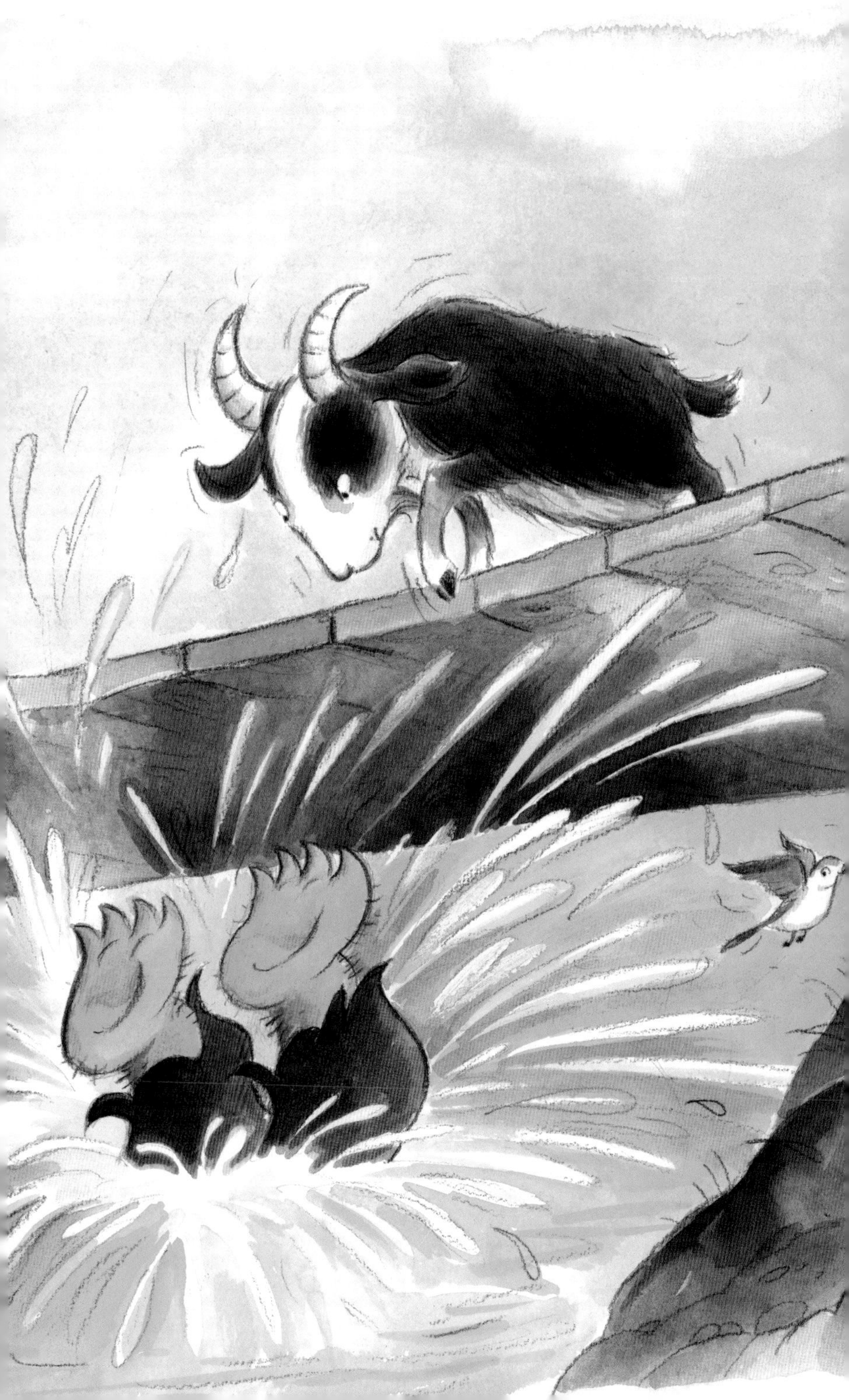

From that time on, people went over the bridge without fear.

Never again did the troll pop his head out from under the bridge to roar, "Who's that trip-trapping over my bridge?"

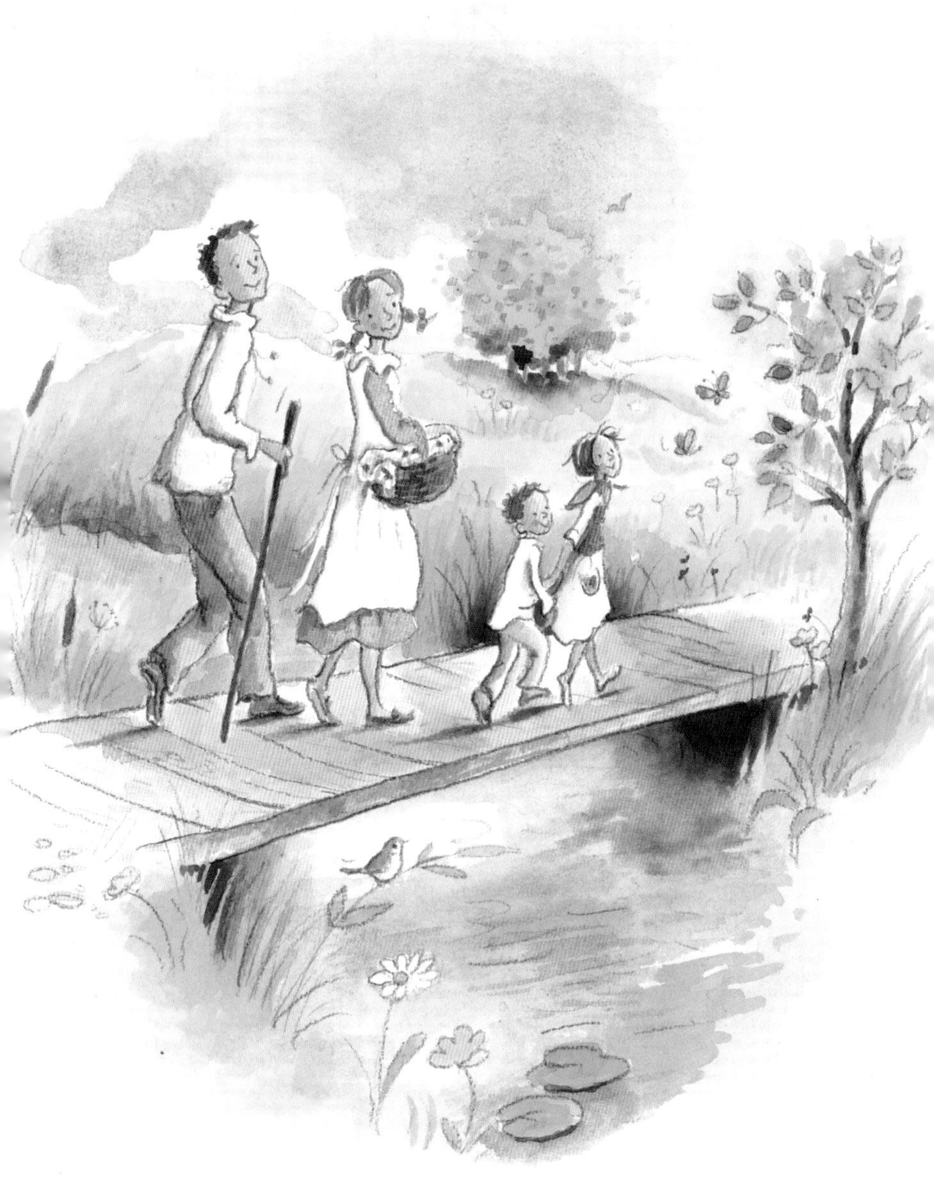

The three billy goats Gruff lived
happily ever after in the meadow
on the hillside. They ate the
sweet grass and they were
never hungry again.

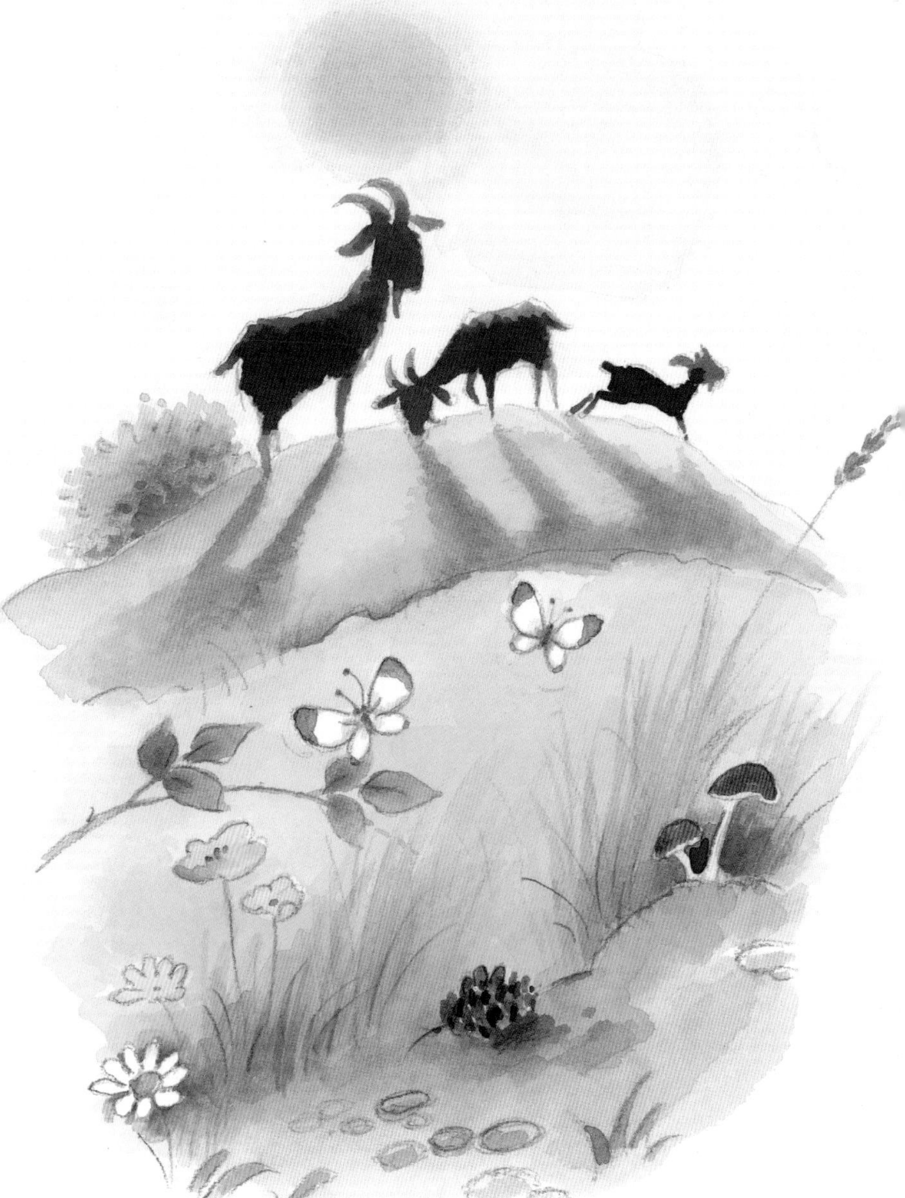

A History of
The Three Billy Goats Gruff

The enduring popularity of *The Three Billy Goats Gruff* has meant that the story has been adapted as a radio play, a TV programme and even a musical.

Although similar stories have been found in other countries, this tale of three goats wanting to cross a river to reach luscious grass is thought to be Scandinavian in origin.

Norwegian writer and scholar Peter Christen Asbjørnsen and Norwegian author Jørgen Moe published the most familiar version of this story in 1845 in their collection *Norske Folkeeventyr*.

The story later appeared in English when George Webbe Dasent translated *Norske Folkeeventyr* as *Popular Tales from the Norse* in 1859.

Ladybird's classic retelling by Vera Southgate has delighted thousands of children, reinforcing the tale's popularity today.

Collect more fantastic

LADYBIRD TALES

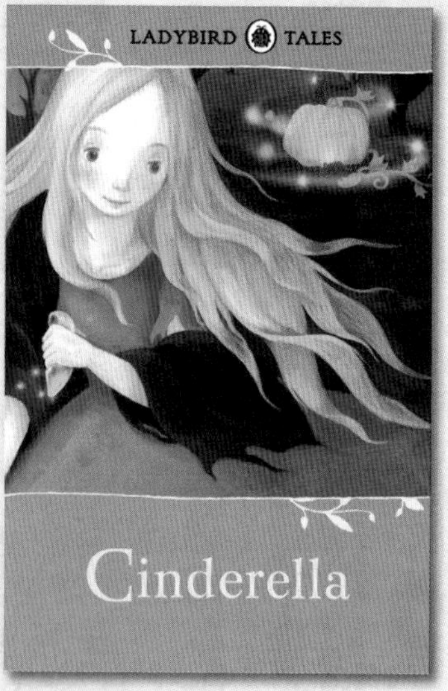
LADYBIRD TALES
Cinderella

9781409311072

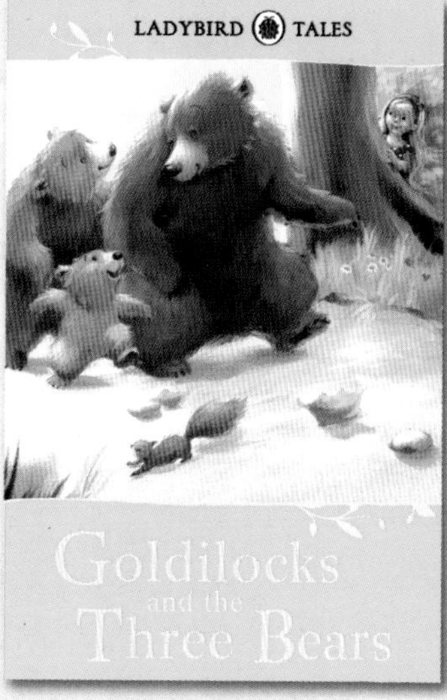
LADYBIRD TALES
Goldilocks
and the
Three Bears

9781409311119

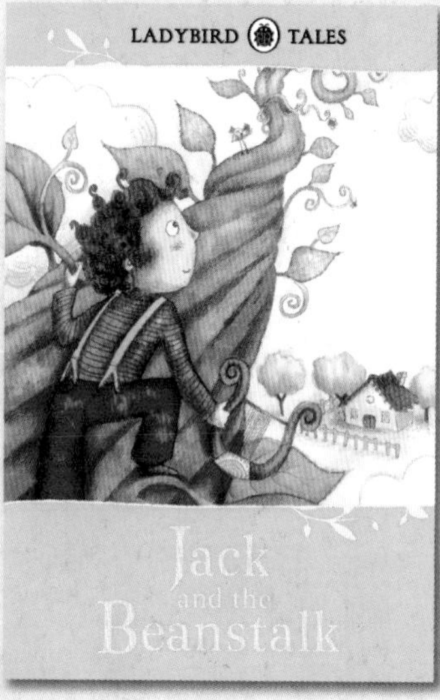
LADYBIRD TALES
Jack
and the
Beanstalk

9781409311102

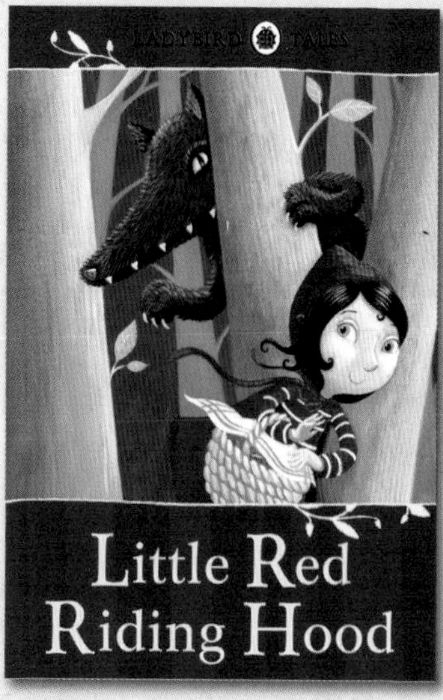
LADYBIRD TALES
Little Red
Riding Hood

9781409311126

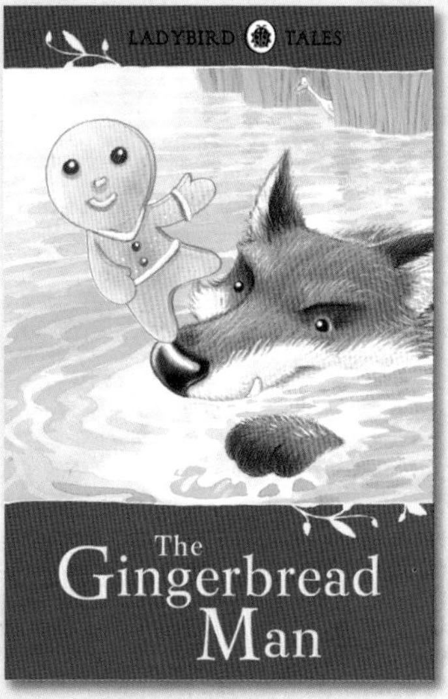
LADYBIRD TALES
The Gingerbread Man

9781409311096

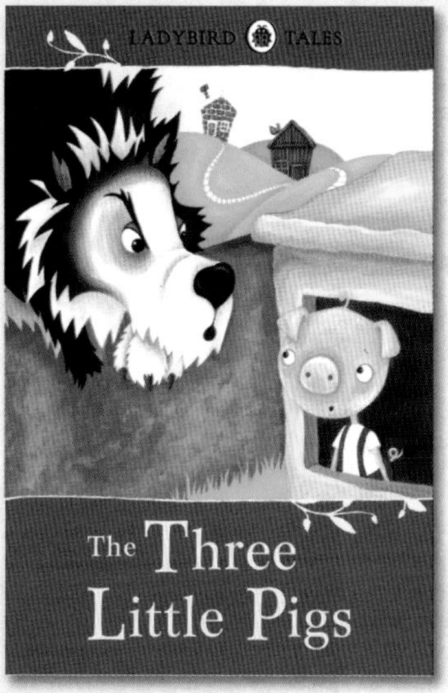
LADYBIRD TALES
The Three Little Pigs

9781409311089

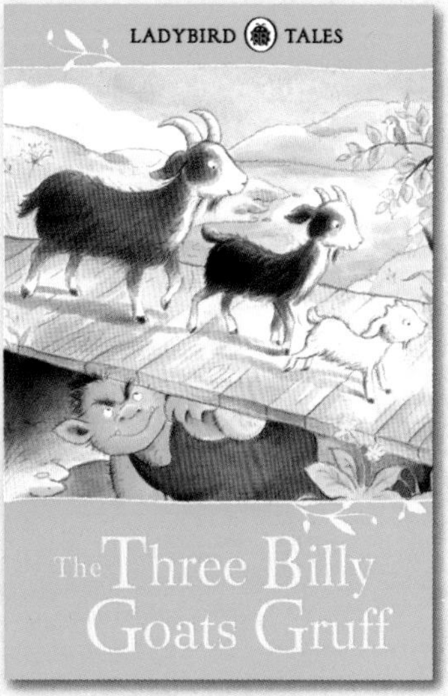
LADYBIRD TALES
The Three Billy Goats Gruff

9781409311065

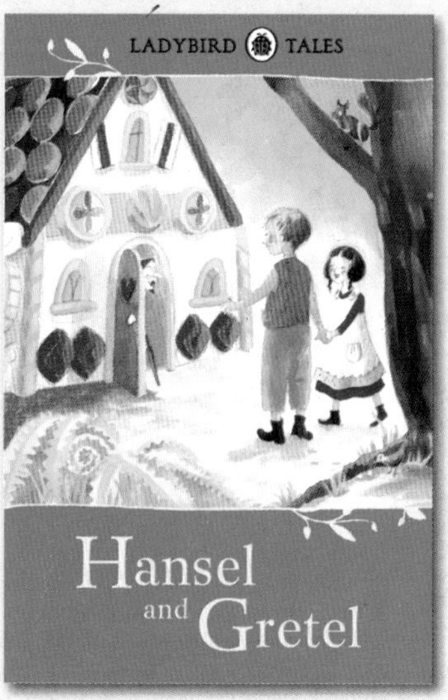
LADYBIRD TALES
Hansel and Gretel

9781409311133

Endpapers taken from series 606d,
first published in 1964

A catalogue record for this book is available from the British Library

Published by Ladybird Books Ltd
80 Strand London WC2R 0RL
A Penguin Company

001 – 10 9 8 7 6 5 4 3 2 1

ISBN: 978-1-40931-106-5

Printed in China

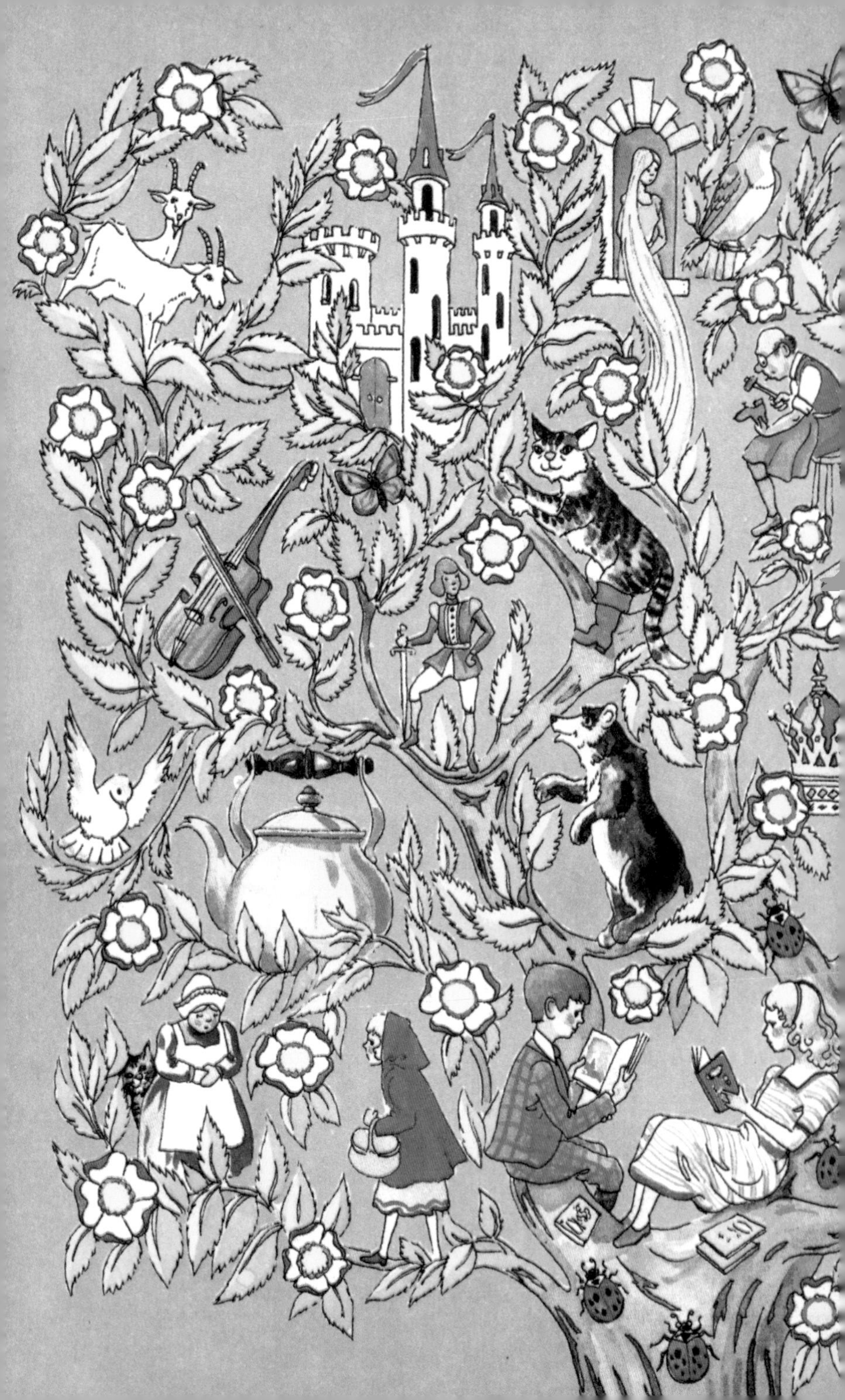